# PROUD T
# A POOPINI

## BY DAVE SINDREY
## ILLUSTRATED BY CHUM MCLEOD

Napoleon Publishing

*To Zachary, Amy and Liam - D.S.*
*To Gianni, for everything - C.M.*

*Text copyright © 1995 David Sindrey*
*Illustrations copyright © 1995 Chum McLeod*

**Published by Napoleon Publishing**
**Toronto  Ontario  Canada**

*Napoleon Publishing gratefully acknowledges the support of The Canada Council.*

**Book design by Cowan Design Inc.**

**Canadian Cataloguing in Publication Data**

Sindrey, David,  1962-
  Proud to be a Poopini

ISBN 0-929141-38-5

1. Picture books for children  I. McLeod, Chum.
II. Title

PS8587.I64P7  1995     jC813'.54     C95-931597-7
PZ7.S55Pr  1995

*Printed and bound in Canada*

Pogo Poopini loved the pogo hotdogs that
they sold at the fair. It was all he ate at home
because...

...Pogo Poopini's family lived at the circus.

At school, though, Pogo Poopini ate egg salad sandwiches and celery sticks and drank milk like all the other kids. Pogo hated egg salad sandwiches, but he ate them anyway because he wanted everyone to think he was normal. "Mmm, mmm, egg salad sandwiches today!" he would say at lunch time.

At school, Pogo Poopini wouldn't wear the sparkly costume that his mother had made him. Pogo wore jeans and T-shirts just like everybody else.

He didn't dare tell anyone about his pet anteater, Lucie, who could walk a tightrope. Pogo was worried that people would think his family was weird.

ne day, Pogo's teacher, Miss Garbonzo, made an announcement. "Uh, excuse me, children. I have an announcement to make," she said. "Tonight is our school's Open House. I hope all of your parents know about it. I'm looking forward to meeting them."

"School Open House!" thought Pogo. He was terrified. "Why didn't anyone warn me?" Pogo was worried that everyone would find out what a weird family he had.

After school, Pogo took his fancy unicycle out of the bushes and rushed straight home to the circus. Posters for the Open House were posted everywhere.

OPEN HOUSE
MEET THE TEACHERS

ALL WELCOME

He hoped that his parents hadn't seen the posters.

**G**ood," he thought, when he got home. "It looks like no one's around." His mother wasn't swinging on the trapeze. His father wasn't climbing buildings. The circus grounds were empty.

No one was around because Pogo's parents had closed the circus. Everyone was waiting for Pogo in the family trailer. "Hi, Pogo. We've closed the circus so that everyone can come to your school's Open House tonight. Even Aunt Marge is coming," said Mrs. Poopini.

"I hope she shaves," thought Pogo.

That evening, all the children in the school came to Open House with their parents. Pogo Poopini was worried. But luckily, his family was acting pretty normally. Aunt Marge hadn't shaved, but she had brushed her beautiful beard and had tied it in braids. Miss Garbonzo complimented Aunt Marge on the pretty pink bows.

Pogo's brother Phil, "The Dog-faced Boy," was lapping up some water from the drinking fountain down the hall. "Please! Don't anyone be weird!" thought Pogo.

"Oh, no!" said Pogo. His uncles Boko and Loko the clowns were juggling the principal over their heads. "Hey... I wonder who those guys are?" said Pogo to a boy beside him.

Everyone went into the auditorium to hear
the principal's speech. Just as everyone had
settled down and the principal had begun to
speak, Pogo's brother Phil stood up and said
"I smell smoke!" Pogo's brother had a great
nose for smells.

"There might be a fire," said the principal.
"Please, no one panic. Everyone move slowly
to the nearest exit. I'll phone the fire depart-
ment." Everyone filed out the nearest exit.

Miss Garbonzo and some of her students
were still on the third floor. Miss Garbonzo
opened a window and leaned out. "I think we
might need some help getting down," she
shouted to the crowd down below.

Miss Garbonzo was right. Smoke was filling
up the classroom. The flames were heading
straight for them. Miss Garbonzo and the
children stayed low to the floor.

Papa Poopini, "The Human Fly," stepped out from the crowd and began to climb up the side of the building. "Oooooooooh, aaaaaaaah!" exclaimed the crowd.  He reached the ledge outside Miss Garbonzo's window and then threw down a rope.

p climbed Pogo's mother, "The Magnificent Martha," best rope acrobat in the world. Gracefully, she began to help each child down the rope.

Suddenly, there was a loud explosion in the room next to them and flames began to pour out the window onto the ledge where Papa Poopini was standing. Thinking quickly, Pogo grabbed his unicycle from the bushes and a garden hose from the janitor.

His pet anteater, Lucie, leapt onto his shoulders and Boko and Loko helped the two of them to the top of the school yard fence. With Lucie holding the hose tightly with her nose, Pogo rode quickly along the top of the fence toward the fire. Lucie aimed the hose and sprayed the water right into the burning window, until the fire retreated. "Hooray!" yelled the crowd.

Magnificent Martha and Papa Poopini helped Miss Garbonzo and all the children safely to the ground and then took a bow.

The firemen came and, after some hard work, they put out the fire.

Boko and Loko made the children laugh and forget how worried they had been. Aunt Marge put an arm around Miss Garbonzo and gave her a coffee.

"Thank goodness for the Poopinis!" said the fire captain.

"You said it!" said the principal. All the children and their parents clapped and yelled.

Pogo gave his Aunt Marge a big hug. He was proud to be a Poopini. "We're proud of you, too," said Aunt Marge. Her whiskers tickled Pogo and made him laugh.